I'm 12 Years Old And I Saved The World

D.K. Brantley

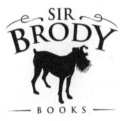

This book is fiction. That said, the names, places, and events in this book are either the product of the author's imagination or are used fictitiously. Any type of resemblance to real life is coincidental, so please don't sue.

Published by Sir Brody Books
Cleveland, Tennessee USA
sirbrody.com

Printed in the United States of America

Cover Art by Vlad C. Diegys

Edited by Rebecca Cochrane

To Jessica, who believed in this book.

To Esther, who gave this book the best compliment possible.

To Leah, who will love this book soon enough.

To Lurlene, who convinced me to write in present tense.

one

I wake up to Mom patting, tapping, pecking my shoulder.

"Adam, Adam. Wake up, Adam. Adam!"

We aren't parked in front of a new bite-sized apartment or government housing like I expected. We're at Grandpa's. It's only a twenty-minute drive from our old house, but yesterday left me physically and mentally exhausted.

I climb out of the car only to realize my legs are still asleep. Suddenly, I'm plunging face-first toward the sidewalk. If not for my lightning-fast reflexes (Hey, who says book nerds don't have hand-eye coordination?), my face would look a little less handsome right now. Thankfully, I've read enough about fast reactions that some of it sunk in.

"Shannon! How good to see you. I guess we'll be roommates now, eh? It'll be great!"

(Quick pause for discerning readers. Yes, I'm a guy. Yes, my name is Adam. And yes, my name is Shannon. Adam Shannon Dakota Carr to be exact. This ridiculous name comes courtesy of my parents, part-time tree-hugging environmentalist greenies. In their sweet environmentalist minds, they decided to choose two gender-neutral names they thought would work whether I was a boy or a girl. Well, they thought wrong. Hence why I go by Adam—an unauthorized addition made by a nurse who wanted me to have a chance at life. Thank you, kind nurse who works in the maternity ward at Plantation Memorial Medical Center. Now…back to the story.)

Roommates? Did Grandpa say roommates?

"Thought we could stay up late talking about girls, stink bombs—all the important stuff."

"Sure, Grandpa."

Deep breath. Last time I stayed at Grandpa's, we did exactly that. We stayed up late talking about girls and stink bombs. Or he talked. I listened and let his rumbling voice put me to sleep as he told stories about childhood pranks gone wrong and how he and Grandma met an eternity ago.

"I should have told you," Mom says once Grandpa is out of hearing distance (which isn't too far, since he's the oldest living person on planet Earth). "Since your dad lost his job, we need to save money, and Grandpa invited us to stay with him."

Mom pauses, grabs my shoulders, and turns my body until I have to face her directly.

"Everything will be fine," she insists. "You may even enjoy sharing a room with Grandpa."

"Sharing a room with him?" I ask. "Sharing a— for how long?"

"I know," Mom says, patting my arm. "It's not easy on any of us. But you either share a room with Grandpa or sleep in the cellar. We figured you'd prefer the bedroom."

"Y'all going to give us a hand, or is this an hour-long pow-wow?"

Mom and I look up, as Grandpa is walking back to the car. Mom has one arm draped over my shoulder and the other rubs my arm as if easing the pain from an invisible boo-boo.

"Yeah, we're coming old man," she says with a fake scowl. "Don't get your panties in a wad!"

With that, she turns and grabs the last bag out of the car trunk. Convinced I'm going to get off without carrying anything in, I turn to survey my new neighborhood.

It's not the worst place in the world. Have a lot of memories here, actually. Good ones, too. Memories of Grandpa pulling me around the block in that lightning-fast red wagon. Memories of Grandma making the most amazing root beer floats a guy could ever want. Memories of Grandma giving Grandpa the stink eye when we came in for dinner looking like we'd just played in a mud pit.

Sure, there is no one in the neighborhood my age. Not kids I can relate to, at least. Kind of hard to find a 12-year-old who has read more literary classics than his teachers. Even harder to find one whose only mobile device is one of those prepaid phones that's programmed to only call one phone number: his mother's cell phone.

Yeah, thanks to my parents' desire to save the world, they're saving me from those evil phones that let you visit the world in the palm of your hand. Because who would want their kid to fit in or have something to do when things get a bit dull? Not my folks. As if my scrawny arms, long hair, and slightly concave chest don't make life hard enough, they stick me with a prepaid, call-Mommy-and-Daddy-only phone.

Well, at least I don't have to carry anything into Grandpa's. Or that's what I think. Until I see a moving truck barrel down the road and come to a stop in front of Grandpa's house.

"We've gotta move all…"

"You're not the only one who'd rather kick back and relax."

Dad stands beside me, staring at the oversized moving truck at the curb. He sighs loudly and promises it won't be as bad as it looks. Sounds like a hollow promise to me, but whatever. We did just get kicked out of our foreclosed house after Dad got laid off from his consulting job, so disappointment is the order of the day.

The next three hours are a blur of brown boxes, guessing which container belongs in what room of Grandpa's house, and wishing for another ten-minute break to suck down some generic electrolyte-replenishing sports drink.

By the time we get to the last row of boxes stacked haphazardly in the back of the truck, I start plotting ways to be lazy. Move slow enough, I scheme, and Mom, Dad, and Grandpa will handle most of the remaining boxes. But my plan doesn't work. Seems the slower I go, the more boxes are left for little old me. It is almost as if I'm the only person doing anything anymore.

"Hey, man."

I spin to face a hulking figure at the back of the truck. The darkness of the truck and the brightness outside play tricks on my eyes. All I see is a massive silhouette, and it doesn't provide enough clues for me to determine if the thing is human or Sasquatch. Its voice reverberates against the metal walls as it lifts a meaty hand.

I try matching my voice to its, but it's futile.

"Hi," comes my high-pitched response.

The thing leans its weight against the truck wall, causing the truck to tilt to the left.

"Moving in?"

"Looks like it," I respond. I instantly hope it doesn't sense sarcasm in my tone. Something that large would not respond well to sarcasm.

"Cool." It peeks its head outside the truck and then back inside at me. "Need a hand?"

If this creature had only been here two hours ago!

"Think I'm good now. Just a couple boxes and

I'm done."

It doesn't budge.

"Thanks though," I finish, my voice still hitting a girlish high pitch.

Its large silhouetted head shakes once, and fast as it arrived, it's gone.

"Mom? Dad?" I listen from inside the moving truck. "Grandpa?"

Silence.

I walk back to the house, following the sound of voices until I find all the responsible adults in my life sitting in the kitchen. Grandpa is on a cushioned straight-back chair at the eat-in kitchen table. Mom is on the countertop, her legs dangling toward the floor. Dad perches on top of a wooden stool Grandpa carved before I was even a thought.

None of them are sweating, and no one's concerned that I'm soaked from head to foot. Don't seem to notice me at all, actually. Not until I clear my throat.

"Adam, dear!" Mom speaks first, giving quick glances at my father and grandfather. "All finished? Want something to drink? You look exhausted."

I sit on a chair beside Grandpa, grab an ice-filled glass from the table, and pour out some blue sports drink. I'm beat, and by the you-look-like-an-exhausted-puppy-dog look I score from Mom, I'm not the only one who knows it.

After fussing my hair, Mom stands up and tosses together a quick peanut butter and jelly sandwich.

"Saw the neighbor kid climb into the truck," Grandpa says. "Guess you met him?"

"Neighbor kid?" I ask, my mouth full of sandwich.

"Yeah—name's Michael. Not sure what the story is," Grandpa says, "but he lives in the old West place with his mom. Big kid. Not sure how old he is."

That hulking thing that wandered into the truck is a human child? What's he eat for breakfast—eighteen-wheelers with a side of killer whale?

"Close your mouth, dear," Mom says. "It's full of food, and I am not interested in seeing any of it."

two

Morning is announced by the sound of a curtain being pulled aside and blinding sunlight.

"Wondering when you'd ever wake up," Grandpa says.

He's already dressed in his Grandpa outfit: tan suit pants, a thin ribbed button-up dress shirt, and brown leather shoes with no laces or socks. The red lights on Grandpa's clock read 6:40 beside his matching twin mattress. Guess I was too tired to care that he was sleeping in the room with me or even to hear his snoring.

When I get to the kitchen, Mom and Dad are sitting down, both wearing suits.

"Busy day today," Dad says. "Mom and I, we've both got job hunting to do. But before that, we've gotta get your school situation figured out."

"Figured out? Am I late again or something?"

Mom looks at Dad, then at Grandpa, and smiles.

"We didn't realize it when we decided to come here to live with your Grandpa, but we're three blocks past the zoning for your old school. You've got to go to Palmetto Middle now."

The concern in Mom's voice equals the hope in my mind. A new school means new people to meet, a chance to reinvent myself into whatever cool cat I want to be.

"Really!" I say with a little too much enthusiasm.

Mom looks at me like my body has been invaded by an alien.

"What? Could be worse," I say. "Just…trying to go with the flow."

Composure back in place, I return to my room and let a smile come to the surface.

A new school? This may be okay after all. Of course, there is the whole sharing-my-bedroom-with-Grandpa thing, but I can deal with that later. Or maybe I won't have to. Maybe old people will be in style at my new school. If that's the case, I'll be the talk of the town.

After brushing my teeth and tossing on some clean duds (those are clothes for those who haven't read any 1950's-era books), I return to the kitchen. A piece of toast and a glass of orange juice stare at me from the counter.

I put up a small fight, but as usual I'm force fed breakfast by my concerned parental units.

Grandpa wraps his hand around my right bicep.

"A boy your age either eats breakfast or stays puny."

"Thanks for the tip, Grandpa."

"And your hair…"

"His hair," interrupts Mom, "is just fine. Long hair doesn't make him a hoodlum. It makes him a free spirit."

If Mom only knew how much I wanted to chop off this free-spirit do for something a bit more—well, clean shaven. Not that I want to be bald, but I dream of a day I'm not constantly pulling hair out of my eyes and mouth.

Grandpa's helpful tip and Mom's defense of how she wants my hair, followed by a glass of post-tooth-brushing orange juice would normally have been enough to make me want to get back in bed. But I have a new school to conquer, and I have high hopes that everyone will love the new kid.

In case you missed it, the new kid is me.

three

Despite my parents' best efforts, getting me into a new school isn't as easy as signing on a dotted line. Dad says it's because no government employee works on Friday. Whatever the real reason, we go from Palmetto Middle to my old school then to the school district's central office. Everywhere we go, we hear the same story: go somewhere else. So instead of beginning my reign as the new kid on the block (not the boy band from the 1980s or the puppet group that teaches good life lessons to young kids), I waste all day in the car, taking a monotonous tour around town.

Granted, I do get to meet one fly honey at Palmetto Middle School: Noelle. She is going to show me around the school. I've figured out some great lines to use on her when some office worker informs my parents that we need to go to the central office. Thanks, office worker.

I outwardly shrug off the interruption of what I know will blossom into a long and marvelous romance, but the slight whimper in my voice gives away my disappointment.

While some would write the entire day off as a loss, I look on the bright side. No, I don't become the coolest new kid ever at my new school. That'll happen tomorrow. But I do get to skip school all day. Even if it is spent in a car with my parents and my ribbed-shirt-wearing Grandpa, it's pretty sweet. And if necessary, I can always spin the story into something a little more glorious for my new classmates.

By the time we get all the school stuff figured out, it's well after 5 p.m. and everyone in the car is in a bad mood. Which means everyone at the house is in a bad mood.

As I reach the front door, I sense something watching me. Across the street, that gigantic creature that is supposed to be a kid is silhouetted again. This time, it's standing at its open front door and I wave back to its big mitt.

AND I SAVED THE WORLD

Seems friendly enough—in a shadowy way—but all I want to do is go to my room, shut the door, and get some privacy.

Unfortunately, I no longer have a bedroom to call my own, the house's two bedrooms border the living room, and Grandpa is enjoying the novelty of having some new faces around the house. So privacy is at a premium.

"After dinner, who wants to watch Jeopardy!?"

In case you don't know, there's no way to tell your granddad you don't want to watch his favorite game shows with him. Besides, if I ditch Jeopardy!'s onslaught of answers for some me-time, I would hear the crowd's cheers, oohs, and aahs from my—our—bedroom, and my curiosity would get the best of me eventually. I am, must I remind you, a rather literate 12-year-old, and I can hold my own in just about any game show out there.

So bring it on, old man.

Who is King Tut?

What is Kuwait?

What is 1933?

What is cobalt?

What is a Dalmatian?

The show isn't even to the first commercial

break, and I'm already smoking Grandpa. Feels pretty good. Especially after a lifetime of suffering through his speech about how ignorant today's generation is.

And then Double Jeopardy! arrives: Particles, Things That Go Bump, 1999, Ways Teens Can Make Money, Black and White, and Begins With "G."

The last-place contestant starts with something easy: Begins With "G." Obviously a rookie trying to get some points. Easy as the subject is, I don't get any of the questions. I don't even pay attention to the answers. All I can think of is Ways Teens Can Make Money.

Ways Teens Can Make Money.

Sure, I'm months away from being a teenager, but give me a break. My mind swirls with ideas, ways I can work my way into financial gain. Not into an absolute fortune, but into more money than I've ever had. Enough money to get a laptop or mp3 player, so I can start downloading music from the last decade.

If I work hard, I can even get enough money to—

In a galaxy far, far away, a familiar robotic jingle sounds, and a man speaks: "Let's make it a true Daily Double, Alex."

The old me would have been intrigued. Not

now. There are more pressing matters. I've got to save the world.

four

You read right. I'm going to save the world. Laugh if you want, but laughing is the last thing on my mind. Okay, I do chuckle a tad at the grandiose plan I concoct. But it is one of those laughs that says, "I've fallen upon a great idea and am amazed that no one else has figured this out before. Then again—I am a genius, so I'm not that surprised."

In case you've not figured it out yet (and I admit I haven't given enough of a clue to fill you in), this hero thing is coming in the form of financial security for my folks. That's right. I'm going to save my family from financial ruin—the ruin that has landed us in Grandpa's house. The ruin that I'm in the middle of right now because my dad, the English-degreed literature lover, turned into some sort of environmental consultant and got fired for his efforts. Actually, he got fired months ago and only told Mom about it when the bills finally caught up to us and we got booted from the house. Must have thought love truly was all he needs.

Anyway…what is this master plan, you ask?

Okay, it's not exactly mapped out to perfection, but I do know a couple things.

Thing # 1 that I know: If it's possible for teens to make money flipping burgers and washing cars, it's possible for pre-teens to make some dough doing stupid stuff for people, too.

Thing # 2 that I know: My parents will never go for it. In their sweet little save-the-world-starting-with-our-son minds, young boys should not fret about finances or anything more worrisome than world peace and saving the trees. If my parents could have their druthers, I'd be sitting around in flower fields singing Kumbaya, while I proclaim the excellence of pre-algebra and incense. Okay, they're not that far gone, but they're firm believers that kids should be kids as long as they can, and that means growing their imaginations via reading and thinking, not working and worrying.

So if I'm going to be the financial hero for my little family, I'm going to have to do it on the down low—the DL—in order to keep my moneymaking ways on track. 'Cause if Mama or Papa Wolf gets scent of my scheming, the jig is up.

Now to figure out how to get started. If I didn't zone out during Double Jeopardy!, I probably could have learned some decent ways to jump-start my business venture.

"These dishes aren't going to wash themselves, Adam."

Mom's voice shakes the dollar bills out of my head.

"All right, Mom." I sigh, stretch my arms overhead, and yawn. "You gonna help me?"

"And just why would I do that?"

"Cause dinner was an hour ago. Those plates are going to be all kinds of crusty." I give my best puppy dog eyes. "Please?"

"Okay," Mom says finally. "But don't think I'll be this easy next time."

With a washcloth in hand and a piece of steel wool within reach, I start scrubbing. Why does Grandpa not invest in a dishwasher? Oh well. At least I can use this time to think of ways to make money.

"Saw how you looked at that girl at Palmetto Middle today."

"Girl?" My face burns.

Guess the whole hero thing will have to wait. Right now, I have to take care of the dishes with a side order of denial.

five

"I've got it!"

Bending over to tie my tennis shoes, I bob my head up and down in a victory dance, letting my hair cover my face.

"What have you got there, son?"

The voice startles me and I peek over my shoulder at Grandpa, who is slipping on his shoes at the same time.

"Oh, nothing, Grandpa. Just thinking of something." To be honest, I forgot I share a bedroom with an elderly man who could be present at any and all times.

But you probably don't care about that. What

you care about is what I "got" that I so easily avoided telling my Grandpa. Well, I figured out my plan for saving my family. After sleeping on it over the weekend, the perfect game plan has formed in my brain, a brain so full of classic novels and *Women's Day* magazine that I'm surprised there's room for something as quaint and ordinary as foolproof ways to make money.

It's simple—though it comes with risks.

Since moving in with Grandpa, I've realized how much stuff he has lying around. There are typewriters from a bygone era, books of postage stamps that look like they existed when the Pharaohs were in power, canes with lion-head handles, and first-edition hardback books dating as far back as 1905. No, I'm not going to steal the stuff. I'm going to convince Grandpa I need it. Then I'll pawn it, stuff the money under my parents' pillow, and be the hero. Like all heroes, I'll get the girl.

The only problem is there is more than one problem. First of all, I've got to convince Grandpa to let go of some of his most beloved possessions. Or what I figure could be his most beloved possessions.

Second, once I convince him to let me have even an old stopwatch, he'll probably expect me to have and hold it for the rest of my life. So if I get rid of something he gives me, it'll be pretty hard to tell him what I did with it. And if I tell the truth, it will probably end the whole he-gives-me-stuff-so-I-can-sell-it thing.

How to get around it?

"Shannon Dakota Carr, it's time for school, buddy. You've got to get going."

Dad, like Mom, has an uncanny ability to stop me in mid-thought.

My first day at Palmetto Middle is typical. As expected, everyone loves me, and I finally get that long-awaited tour with Noelle. Now, I know some guys are into the whole blonde-hair, blue-eye thing, but give me a brunette any day of the week. One preferably with the curly long hair Noelle has, her sense of straightforward unflashy style, and that quiet demeanor that makes her attention worth so much.

Anyway, while being the new kid is great, it isn't without its awkward moments.

"Class, you've all noticed by now that we have a new student."

Mr. Pendergrass—better known as The Glowing Orb, stands in front of the classroom. He couldn't be older than 25, but his lack of hair pushes him deep into the next decade. Of course, his everyday dull attire doesn't help.

"I'd like you to all welcome," he continues, taking a long pause as he scours his roll book, "Adam Shannon Dakota Carr. Do you go by…"

An invisible rope tightens on my neck for the briefest moment. But I've been through the routine and play it cool.

"I go by Adam, sir."

"Very good. Have a seat, Adam, and we'll get to work."

Repeat this six more times, substituting The Glowing Orb with a variety of everyday teachers who have everyday teacher personalities and everyday teacher expectations, and you've got my first day at Palmetto Middle, wrapped up with a nice bow on top.

Pack on all the new knowledge I gain (such as the obvious fact that Palmetto Middle School's abbreviation is PMS and school colors are red and white), homework in five out of seven classes, and the realization that Noelle is way out of my league, and my weariness at 3 p.m. becomes understandable.

Now, if I can just rip through this homework, I'll

be able to devote some brainpower to the real problem at hand: making money. I know I can't just start yanking stuff off the fireplace mantel and pawning it, but I also can't sit around thinking for the rest of my life. Something's gotta give.

That knock means the something will have to give later. Mom looks at me from the doorway. I look down and realize I've not flipped open my history book yet, though I've been sitting in front of it for at least 20 minutes.

Mom raises an eyebrow.

"All right, all right. I'm on it, Mom. Napoleon, here I come!"

She feigns excitement, storms across the small living room, and resumes cooking something that smells too good for me to focus on a long-dead, rather short Frenchman.

Hungry as the scents make me, I need to figure out this Napoleon guy. Because as great as *Bill & Ted's Excellent Adventure* is, I'm pretty sure it's lacking historic accuracy.

six

This is where my story skips ahead a bit. Because as fun as it may be to recount the endless math, science, history, English, PE, Spanish, and typing classes I sit through—make that suffer through—it wouldn't serve much purpose for my story. Because this is a heroic story.

Oh yeah—before I forget it, don't think I "suffer through" my classes like some kind of martyr, moaning and groaning nonstop. I use my time wisely. Every time the teacher goes over something I already know, I let my mind wander to the true issue at hand: making cash. And since PMS (yeah, it took me a while to get used to calling it that, too) isn't known for its academic rigor, I have plenty of that special mind-wandering time on my hands.

However, there are advances worth noting.

Case in point: Noelle.

Strangely enough, I don't realize how far I'd fallen for her. So far, in fact, that she replaced all the heart throbs at my old school. Grandpa knows about it, too. And he lets me know it bright and early one morning at breakfast.

He's sitting bolt upright in his signature see-through ribbed button-up shirt, eating a bowl of oatmeal or whatever else old people eat to keep themselves healthy and "regular."

"Noelle? Just a girl at school," I say in a voice not quite as casual as I desire. "Why?"

"Oh," Grandpa says between sips of orange juice. "You talked about her last night."

He takes another sip, eying me, letting his words take effect. And they indeed have effect. A pretty dog-gone creepy effect.

Finally, I admit I don't remember talking about Noelle. "Don't know why I would," I add.

"Oh," he says. "We weren't talking about her. You talked about her in your sleep."

"My sleep?" The top of my head glows red-hot.

Did I dream I was in class next to her, asking for a pencil? Or were we holding hands on the Riviera? Oh no. It was a kiss. It was definitely a kiss.

"That's weird," I finally say, the knot in my throat making each word stutter out painfully. Before I can wonder whether I'd said anything in my sleep about the dream kiss she planted on me, Grandpa interrupts my thoughts.

"Guess you're done with Jennica now?"

"Jennica?"

"Talked about her the first few weeks we bunked together." Grandpa laughs a knowing, taunting laugh. "Happens all the time, Adam. Nothing to be ashamed of. Guy gets a gal on the brain and she won't leave him alone. Even when he's trying to get some shut eye."

Concentrating so hard I could feel my brows closing in on my eyes, I finally remember Jennica. I picture her short brown hair as it fell out from behind her ears, where she tried unsuccessfully to keep it tucked. Where is Jennica now? Would she even remember me? Why had I always been afraid to even speak to her?

"You know, I'll always be here if you want to talk girls," Grandpa says with a wink. He puts his glass and bowl in the sink and heads into the house's only bathroom. It will be a while before he takes care of his morning routine, and I've not brushed my teeth yet. Win some, lose some.

Even worse: Grandpa knows about my lady issues. And if I talk about Noelle in my sleep, I may have let something slip about my master plans for saving my world from destruction.

Then again, maybe letting him know about it isn't such a bad idea.

No, that's crazy talk.

But maybe it is worth it to pitch the idea to him. He may be game, interested in helping the cause.

Come on, what am I thinking?

Okay…but I have to be smooth. Very smooth. "Need in here?"

Grandpa walks out of the bathroom, leaving a series of wavy lines in his wake. You know—the ones in cartoons that let you know something stinks? Yeah. They're definitely there.

Unfortunately, I have to get in there to brush my teeth, so I don't have a choice.

School today isn't the worst ever, but it could have been better.

AND I SAVED THE WORLD

"Hey, check this out!"

A group of students gather around at the prodding of the biggest kid in sixth grade, who looks vaguely like the silhouette that stood at the back of the moving van. It's a routine I grew weary of at my old school, but one with potential perks.

"Who was the eighteenth president?" he asks.

Everyone freezes, mouths slack, eyes bulging at the thought that someone would have access to such knowledge. Their stares dare me to answer. Getting it right isn't the hard part. Knowing how they will respond is. Will they hate me for knowing more than they do or use me like some sort of electronic parrot? Will I become the person to sit beside in class for cheating purposes?

Doesn't matter. By now they know I know and I know I have to let them know I know they know I know and don't mind.

"Ulysses S. Grant..."

I say it plainly, matter-of-factly, but cap it off with some hint of a question mark. Lets them think I'm not exactly sure.

Before I gauge their reaction, the big kid is at it again.

"Told you! Probably knows more than all of us

put together. Craziest part about it all," he continues, "he doesn't even need Google!"

I smile sheepishly. Relative obscurity is now impossible at PMS. But that's fine. Being buddy-buddy with a caveman does come with benefits. Protection, for one.

I look him in the eye with a knowing smirk.

"What's Google?" I ask.

"What's Google?" He looks blankly at me, tilts his head, and eventually howls with laughter. "What's Google!" he repeats, pounding his larger-than-average-sixth-grader hand on my back. "Ha! What's Google!"

He wraps his beefy arm around my thin back and begins walking out of the crowd that had gathered to watch the new kid answer questions.

"You're all right," he says, looking down at me. "Stick with me. I'll take care of you."

As we begin to part the crowd like Moses through the Red Sea, an anonymous voice pipes up.

"How'd you know he knew all that stuff?"

The big kid turns around to face his questioner and smiles.

"I didn't, but he lives across the street from me, so yeah—not surprising. Everyone on my street is a genius."

A couple days later, I find out the big kid's name is Michael Jackson. Yeah. Michael Jackson. He goes by Big Mike, though, so nobody cares that he can't moonwalk, sing well, or make millions of people scream and pull their hair out at his mere presence.

Now that I got the hang of PMS, I don't have to suffer the pains of being dropped off by my parents. It's back to riding the bus, a.k.a. The Big Cheese. Sitting a row behind me and turned sideways on his bench, unbuckled: Big Mike—the neighborhood ogre I'm in the process of becoming attached to.

When the bus squeaks to a stop at my place, he climbs off, too, and starts trekking toward his house across from Grandpa's.

"See ya tomorrow!" he yells.

"Don't forget to study for that math quiz," I reply.

Big Mike answers with the smirk that I already recognize as his trademark look.

seven

While life is peaches and cream at PMS and I've befriended the biggest dude at school (yes, Big Mike is larger than anyone in sixth, seventh, or eighth grade), things aren't so peachy keen at the house. For one thing, we've been living with Grandpa for three months, and there are no signs that anything is going to change any time soon. Each day, Dad's routine becomes more routine and less hopeful. He wakes up, gets dressed in his business suit and tie, and settles into the couch at Grandpa's house, where he sits by the phone, praying for it to ring. Or if he's not heard back from anyone in a while, he hits the road, asking receptionists when he can come in for an interview.

How he maintains a relatively positive attitude through it all, I don't know. On occasion, he acts so strangely content that I wonder if he's doing other things some of the more extreme environmentalists are known for. But if there is one thing I know about my dad, it's that he walks a path as straight as his neck-tie, so there is no chance he's using illicit substances.

Dad's not the only one off his rocker. Mom cries almost every day, and the slightest thing sets her off. Burned toast? She starts crying. News story about a dog that needs a good home? Here come the tears. Thinking about our old house? Bawling.

She's also getting snappy with Dad.

"What do you mean there are no jobs out there in your line of work?"

"I mean there are no jobs in my field."

"Then do something else! Use that English degree you paid so much for!"

It's a conversation I hear time and again, at various volumes and tones.

Sometimes the question-and-answer session lasts only seconds. Afterward, Mom falls silent and Dad walks out of the house and sits on the front steps.

At other times, it goes on for what seems like hours. One question comes right after another, accusations fly, someone says something I shouldn't hear, and then the silence.

Thursday morning I wake up early to answer the call of my bloated bladder. I take the two steps through the living room to get to the bathroom, relieve myself, scrub my hands, and head back to bed when something on the couch catches my eye. Something lumpy and large.

At the top of the lump is dad's head. I suspect he fell asleep watching television, but the TV isn't on.

In third period that day, I finally make sense of the whole thing. Dad didn't fall asleep on the couch while watching TV. He'd not fallen asleep there on accident.

My heart beats in my ears. My breathing stops. I double over from sudden, overwhelming stomach pain. The teacher in front of the room, rattling off answers to last night's homework, is inaudible. Through my thumping heart, I can't escape the thought:

Dad slept on the couch because he didn't want to be close to Mom.

eight

Now I have to save my parents' marriage? I've barely started on the financial thing and the new school stuff is still throwing me for a loop. Now my entire family's future is lodged in my hands?

So I've got two bigger-than-middle-school issues to deal with. Fail at one, fail at both. Without romance, there's no need for money. Without money, no chance at romance. So I have to kill two birds with one stone or toss two stones at the same time or… well, you get the point.

Then Grandpa has to show up and ruin my thought process…again.

"Sir?"

"It's fall, and you know what that means, don't you?"

I squint at the ceiling fan blades spinning lazily overhead. Allergies? Mold? The flu? Love? Is that what he wants to hear? Love? I look at Grandpa.

"Er...Love?"

"Ha-ha, my boy! That's the spirit! Love isn't just for the spring!" He pats me on the back with Big Mike-like force. "Sadly, there's something else we need to deal with right now. Yard's gotta be mowed so all those dead leaves get mulched up. I thought you'd be just the guy for the job."

Cutting grass? Another kink in the plan.

"Mower's in the garage out back."

I toss on my oldest cut-off jean shorts and walk toward the garage when Big Mike shows up.

"What ya doing?" His big voice still unnerves me a bit, but I keep it together pretty well.

"Grandpa wants me to cut the grass, so—yeah. You give me a hand with this garage door?"

Big Mike reaches down and grabs the large garage door handle, gives it a spin, and pulls. It rotates up easily but doesn't stay that way. Fortunately, a broom falls out of the garage.

I use the broomstick to prop open the door and

look in. It's pitch black, and there is no sign of a light switch. So I stare into the great garage abyss until my eyes adjust.

"Whoa!" Big Mike says, as he leans into the darkness. "This is cool!"

His eyes must have adjusted in a different time period than mine, because there is nothing "cool" in my line of sight.

Stuck behind mounds of ancient junk is a mower that was probably pushed around by Druids keeping the lawn in good shape around Stonehenge. There's no pull string to start the motor, no protective plastic thing hanging from the back to keep my toes from being chopped off. Just a handle attached to three crooked blades.

Big Mike pushes on a small stack of boxes while I fight to pull the mower out of the garage. Eventually I win the battle. But not before I tip over a bucket full of rancid liquid and almost grab a saw by the blade.

"I'm outta here!"

Hand over his nose, Big Mike tromps down the driveway and away from whatever that scent is coming from. Left alone, I ease the mower down the driveway and watch the blades spin one over the other. It does look kind of cool—I'll give Mike that. Now to see how this baby works!

Ever mowed grass? Try doing it with a mower from the Flintstones. It may look idealistic and quaint, but it's not easy. You've got to go over every blade of grass at least three times, and even then there's no guarantee it will actually get cut—especially if you have Big Mike-sized leaves in the way. And that little metal mower is heavy. Very heavy.

By the time I finish mowing the yard, I look like I took a shower with my clothes on. I drip sweat through the living room and into the kitchen, grab a glass of ice water, and collapse into a kitchen chair. Dad and Grandpa stop their conversation to stare me down.

"What have you been doing?" Dad asks.

"I asked him to cut the grass," Grandpa says as I drain my glass, "but I'm not quite sure what he did to get that way."

"What I did to get this way?" I say with ice between my teeth. "I mowed the grass."

"Whose grass? My yard only takes ten or fifteen minutes. You do the whole neighborhood?"

I look at Dad. No sign of understanding.

"Ten minutes? Who are you kidding? That old thing is almost impossible to work!"

"Old thing?" Grandpa says. He walks to the front door and laughs.

"Come here, boy."

I follow Grandpa to the garage. He walks past the large front door to a small door on the side and flips a light switch.

Directly at my feet is a sparkling, yellow lawnmower that looks like it's never touched a blade of grass.

I shake my head and rub my temples.

"Didn't know there was another door over here," I say. "And I couldn't see very well."

"Well, you can use this one next time."

"That won't be necessary," Dad says.

No more mowing? Dad saves the day again!

I smile at Dad. He's still in his coat and tie—just in case an interview comes up. He looks sharp, and his insistence that I don't have to mow the yard is proof that he's thinking sharply as well. I'm about to tell him this when he cuts in.

"He can use the reel mower."

"The what?"

"Reel mower," Dad said. "R-e-e-l. It's the thing you used today. Good to learn how to use stuff from the good old days. Besides," Dad continues, "it's better for the environment."

Once again, Dad's environmentalist leanings show up just in time to make life a little bit worse.

A phone rings in the distance.

"Could be a job!" Dad says crazily, sprinting to the house.

Grandpa grabs my shoulder. I turn toward him as he reaches out his free hand. I shake it.

"Good job out there," he says. "Looks like it did when your Dad used to cut it."

I laugh at the thought of Dad sweating his way across the lawn back and forth, over and over, sweat drenching his shirt and his shorts, falling down his face, rolling off his nose.

"Here's a little something for your efforts." Grandpa reaches into his pocket, pulls out a $20 bill. "Want to make a little more?"

nine

A hard knock on the bathroom door startles me.

"Hey! I'm in here!" I shout. "Just trying to dry off!"

"Oh, sorry…"

"Mike?"

"Yeah." He pauses. Pauses a little longer. "It's me. Adam?"

If it was cool to hug guys who make you laugh, I'd hug that brute right now. Well…if I wasn't in the bathroom. Or drying off. Or…you get the point.

"Wanna come over for dinner? Mom says it's okay."

*****

I'M 12 YEARS OLD

My wet hair sits on my shirt collar as we walk across the street and into Mike's house. The front door opens to the living room, and a streak of light across the floor leads us to the eat-in kitchen, where his mom sets out a gigantic bowl of potatoes.

"Michael, get to the sink and wash up," she says before she spots me behind Big Mike's bigness. "So good to have you here tonight, Adam! Sit down," she says, gesturing to a chair. "Would have had you earlier, but things have been a bit busy here."

Mike dries his hands and grabs a couple glasses of milk, puts one in front of me and keeps one for himself.

"Milk okay?" he asks.

"Sure thing."

The meatloaf is crazy good. Mrs. Jackson doesn't bake ketchup on the top like they do in the school cafeteria or add weird green stuff like Mom. And that bowl of mashed potatoes? She knows what she's doing. Maybe that's why her son is Big Mike instead of just Mike.

I'm not sure what I expected from the event, but Mike and his mom are remarkably normal. After dinner, Mike shows me around. His room is what you'd expect from a middle-school boy's bedroom. Dirty and a little bit stinky. The rest of the house is typical as well, though it's hard to tell as there are almost no lights on.

We return to the living room and I check out a photo hanging on the wall. A much smaller version of Mike looks back at me through toddler eyes, surrounded by his mom, who looks the exact same, and a large-framed guy.

"Ha! This you, Mike? Proof positive you were the size of a normal human being at one time!"

Big Mike smiles and laughs.

"Yeah, I wasn't born with these muscles," he says, flexing for my benefit.

Feeling puny once again, I turn back to the picture.

"And this your dad? You look just like him!"

I look at Big Mike. He doesn't look back. Mrs. Jackson walks in, looking like she just got horrible news.

"Mike's dad passed away a couple years ago," she says. "We miss him a lot." She joins Mike in his floor staring for a moment before looking up. "We'd love to have you over again soon," she says quietly.

I take the hint, thank her for the meatloaf, bumble an apology for bringing up Mike's dad, and walk in a trance to Grandpa's.

ten

Months into this thing, I've not gotten anywhere with my moneymaking master plan. Then Grandpa has a little laugh at my lawn-mowing, leaf-mulching expense, and I'm in business.

Now to find some more things I can do around the house for a little cash. I mean, I could canvas the neighborhood with that dinosaur of a lawn mower, and I'd likely get a job or two from people who feel sorry for me, but why go to the extra effort? Mowing season is practically over. Besides, I've got a relatively helpless old man at my disposal. May as well make the most of him.

But I can't be too obvious about it. I'll have to

be willing to take some risks, do some work I'm not sure I'll get paid for, and just hope he'll toss another buck or two my way.

Between lunches (also known as the rest of the school day), I do my thing. I make straight A's, but it's not exactly rocket science. Don't believe me? You've not stepped foot in an American middle school lately. And even if it were rocket science, who would care? Mom would still be busy figuring out which cheese is truly made from the happiest cows on planet Earth, and Dad would have his shirt and tie on, ready for a chance at that elusive interview.

Speaking of jobs and my quest to keep my own personal planet from complete devastation, I'm keeping pretty busy at home. Kind of weird calling Grandpa's place home, but hey, for now, home is where you rest your head or something like that. *Better Homes & Gardens* will back me up on that.

For starters, I change the light bulb on the front porch. It was a normal white bulb, and the amount of bugs that hovered around that thing at night would give anyone the willies. So I do Grandpa a solid and switch it with a yellow bulb I found while rummaging through the garage. According to *Real Simple* magazine, yellow bulbs are supposed to be less attractive to bugs.

Then I take his area rugs outside and beat them to oblivion. Some magazine mom had lying around a few years ago said to do this at least once a year, and if the scent of those things is any indication, they've not been cleaned since before the Industrial Revolution. Knocking decades of dust out of those rugs sends me into something of a sneezing fit, but the dust-induced noise is helpful. There is no way Grandpa can ignore my efforts after belting out a baker's dozen worth of sneezes.

"Sneeze any more and your eyeballs are gonna pop out, boy!"

I look at Grandpa through watery eyes and sneeze again. I'm not sure whether I'd be more amazed or horrified at my eyeballs popping out of my head, but I do know that if someone else's eyeballs popped out, I'd want to be there.

After two more sneezes, I wipe my nose and speed walk to the bathroom for a bit of clean up.

From the living room, Grandpa yells, "Blow that stuff outta there!"

Well, good sir, that's exactly what I'm doing. Getting these boogs "outta there."

And so go my days at home, one after another, slowly and silently (well—except for the sneezing), working my way around the house, seeking out small jobs that need doing and simply doing them, hoping the money train will stop at my station again.

At some point, I fear I'll run out of things to do. Despite a lifetime of hatred for all things housework, knowing that these silly chores could keep my family in one piece helps me overcome the desire to sit down and do nothing like the old days.

But I really need to get some dough for my efforts. Because while I've buried myself in physical labor, Dad is still sleeping on the couch and Mom is still walking around with mascara staining her post-crying face.

"Mr. Carr? Did you hear me?"

The Glowing Orb jolts me back to English class, where we're working on the difference between nouns and pronouns. Since I mastered this in—oh, second grade or so—I don't feel the need to pay attention. For some reason, The Orb feels differently.

"Umm, yes, sir," I say, scanning the room. There in the front row is the best gift I could hope for: Big Mike. He discreetly holds up seven thick fingers and mouths, "Seven."

Looking down at my grammar book, I scan the page for number seven.

"The noun is Franklin, the pronoun…his."

"Very good, Adam." The Orb sounds disappointed, but goes on. "Okay, number eight—Alex?"

Where was I? Right before the underpaid, overworked Glowing Orb interrupted my thoughts, I was on the precipice of genius. Something to do with getting Mom and Dad out of the house and on the town for a hot date.

The bell rings before I can remember the details. And focusing is impossible when there are thirty slightly smelly sixth graders fighting to be first out of a room. I'll have to sleep on it and hope the plan comes to me by morning.

eleven

Hot dog! It works! My plan to get my parents to think of something happier than...well...not having any money and living with Dad's dad solidifies itself in my brain while I sleep.

"Looks like somebody woke up on the right side of the bed today, eh?"

It's Grandpa. My jostling must have waked him. Or maybe he's been lying awake in bed for an hour, hoping to hear me say something else embarrassing in my sleep. (Creepy thought, yes, but I can't help but be suspicious.)

"A good day, indeed," I say confidently. "It's Friday!"

AND I SAVED THE WORLD

I hop out of bed and waltz out of the room. As I turn the corner and slide into the bathroom, the lump on the couch shuffles. Dad isn't sleeping well. If all goes as planned, that will change soon.

Following a rushed bathroom routine, I sneak out of the bathroom and tiptoe across the living room. Draped across Grandpa's favorite chair—a brick-hard, tall-and-straight chair covered with something that looks like it came from the Ming Dynasty—are Dad's suit pants.

Yes, he sleeps with nothing on but his undies. And this morning, his nighttime underwear-only habit plays to my advantage. Slowly, carefully, holding my breath, I take the wadded up twenty-dollar bill I earned from mowing and drop it into the front left pocket of Dad's slacks.

I know what you're thinking: "That was the master plan?" Well...yeah. It kind of is, for now. I've been holding that twenty for months, and it's not doing me any good. May as well toss it to a guy in need of some cash.

Besides, you ever grabbed your winter coat and found some cash in it? It doesn't matter if it's a hundred-, twenty-, or even a one-dollar bill. It's like you just won the lottery, found some free cash. Suddenly, the boredom of daily life floats away and nothing remains but absolute joy! If I can give Dad that kind of happiness—even for a moment, it will be a major win. Especially if his joy results in Mom getting some happy time, too.

So laugh if you want, but if it works for me—the smartest kid in this book who is going to save the world—then it'll probably work for my parents, who are responsible for making me the smart kid that I am.

Now that I set up my family for a happy reunion in the afternoon, it's time to head to school.

School is okay. Well, the academic part is at least. I wouldn't exactly describe the social side of things as "okay." It is—how you say…amazing?

Yes, you read right. My social life takes a major boost today. It all starts when I find out we're having a pop quiz in geography. Doesn't sound like something that could give a guy like me a foot forward in the social world, does it? Well, Mr. World—he actually asks us to call him this made-up name—demands students use a number two pencil in his class. Anyone who uses a pen automatically loses 20 points off the assignment. Since I'm not interested in losing points because of some dumb rule made up by an aging teacher who goes by a fake name, I keep a massive stash of those precious number twos in my locker. Every time I head to geography, I grab a small handful, just in case one or two break on me. Not that they ever have. But hey, a guy's gotta be prepared.

When Mr. World announces the pop quiz, I smartly pull out a pair of fresh pencils and walk to the front of the room. While standing at the door, grinding my once-pristine pencils into fine-tipped quiz-killing machines, I glance to the second row. Noelle, my dark-haired princess, is hurriedly opening and reopening her notebooks, backpack, and purse. This damsel in distress obviously forgot or lost her number two pencil.

Thankfully, I'm there with my knight outfit on. I won't let my beloved suffer at the hands of this cruel, cruel World. So I casually sharpen my second pencil and slip it into the slot on top of Noelle's desk as I return to my seat. She looks up, mouths "Thank you," and stuffs the contents of her purse back where it belongs.

"Thank you..."

I see the words mouthed a billion times. I imagine myself opening doors, laying my coat over a mud puddle, pushing Noelle out of the path of a runaway car, holding her hand. After each imaginary event, the same sweet words ooze from her lips.

"Thank you."

All day long and even on the bus, Big Mike is nowhere to be found. Not sure where he is, but it's no big deal. Everyone knows I'm friends with the big guy and no one wants on his bad side, so I get a good seat on the bus even in his absence. Actually, it may be a good thing he's not around. Keeps me from explaining why I'm so giddy.

By the time I get home, I'm riding so high that I'm whistling—something I forsook a few years ago as a sign of immaturity.

"What's gotten into you?"

Mom looks at me, mouth open, a tinge of mascara running down her face.

I laugh and whistle another note for good measure. Okay, the extra note is to buy time. I need to think of something appropriate to tell her. And no— admitting that my crush said "Thank you" for handing her a pencil before a pop quiz in geography isn't going to cut it.

"Yeah," I start. "Guess I just dig this weather. Finally cooling off."

"Finally cooling off?"

Fantastic. Dad's now in the conversation. While I may be able to pass off a quick one-liner to always-crying Mom, Dad isn't buying it.

"Shannon," Dad says, "it's been 'cooling off' for a while. Look outside, son. That half foot of snow isn't there because it's cool. It's cold."

"Well," I say. "I just—I can still like the weather, right?"

"Sure you can, son. Sure." Dad looks suspicious. Like he knows there's something beneath my weather fascination. Well, as you know, there is something else there. But I'm not telling him that.

Exciting as the afternoon begins, the evening is rather nondescript. I do my homework, which is more difficult than usual. Mostly because I doubt the answer to any of my math problems is Noelle, though I almost write it a half dozen times. After struggling through basic math homework, I find one of Grandpa's specialties waiting for me: sloppy Joe. If you're unfamiliar with it, imagine chunky, meaty spaghetti sauce dumped on a couple pieces of bread. Some call it hideous. Grandpa calls it dinner. Sound good? Then I'll give you a call the next time Grandpa gets gourmet.

Once I wipe the last bit of sloppy off my chin

and smoke Grandpa in Jeopardy!, I toodle around a bit, read a chapter of *Ender's Game*, and head to bed.

With visions of Noelle dancing in my head, I drift closer and closer to sleep when it feels like a lead balloon lands on my chest. I can't breathe and I start sweating. The twenty I placed in Dad's pocket went unnoticed. Or at least unmentioned. Did he find the money? Did he think he'd absentmindedly left it in his pocket, wadded up, months ago? Did he imagine some little money fairy had left it there just for him?

I hop out of bed and sprint into the living room. No twenty-dollar bill in sight. Dropping to my knees, I scan under the couch. Nothing there but a few pennies, a knotted strand of string, and a piece of fossilized chocolate.

"You okay, son?"

"Uh, yeah, Dad," I say. "Thought I left something in here. I'll find it tomorrow."

Convinced Dad found the money but didn't have time to celebrate between job interviews, I get back in bed. The money isn't lost, but Dad isn't excited enough about the find to shout about it.

Maybe next time...

twelve

The oversized ring is mesmerizing. Big Mike paws it and holds it up to the light.

"Pretty nice, eh?" Grandpa asks.

Worn from years of wear and tear, "Class of 1960" is barely visible around the blue, shiny stone in the center. A tennis racket, baseball bat, and open school book can barely be made out on the sides. It's clear that whoever earned the ring performed on the athletic field and in the classroom. An impressive feat to someone like myself who doesn't know the difference between a slider and a curveball.

"Thought about selling it a while ago," Grandpa says, taking the ring from Mike. Grandpa heads to the living room, Mike and I in tow. "After wearing it for 45 years, it kind of loses its luster. Especially when I've not picked up a tennis racket or baseball bat for 30—make that 40-plus years. Besides," he grunts as he takes a seat on the couch, "your Grandma was the one who liked it. Wearing it with her gone, it just doesn't feel the same."

"That's yours?"

"Why your eyes so big, boy? Your grandfather hasn't always been a decrepit old man. No sir," he continues, pushing his chest out. "I use to be hot stuff. Didn't even snore back then!"

I laugh, hungry to know more about this mysterious athletic and academic old man who sat before me. How could I be related to him when my parents and I are so weirdly unathletic?

"So you were a baseball player? And a tennis player?"

"Not a player, son. I was a star! A big enough star to get the attention of the finest lady at school."

"Really?" Mike asks. "A star?" He leans forward, arms crossed, hands massaging the bulk of his biceps. I reach for mine and find nothing.

I picture Grandpa in his ribbed button-up shirt, knocking the baseball over the fence. He rounds third base as a beautiful girl cheers him on from the stands. She has dark, curly hair and looks like...Noelle? I shake my head.

"The finest girl?" I ask nervously. "What was she like?"

I pray she didn't have dark, curly hair and honey-brown eyes.

"Oh, she was something else," Grandpa says. "Blonde hair so light it was almost white!"

Whew! Not even close to Noelle. It's Grandma. I picture her and my granddad standing side by side after a big game, both of them wrinkled and wearing the white hair of the elderly.

"You know who that young lady was?"

I do indeed. And it's not disturbing—unlike my visions of Noelle waiting for Grandpa at home plate.

"I'm not sure," I say, giving Grandpa the satisfaction of answering.

"Was it Adam's grandma?"

Thank you, Mike, for ruining a Hallmark moment.

"Smart man, Mike! It was indeed none other than Adam's beloved grandmother—my wife of fifty-one years."

"Fifty-one years? That's a lot of love!"

"You better believe it, Mike. And, Adam, before you try to figure out how we were married that long, I'll tell you something your parents would not want you to know. We got married straight out of high school. She was 17. I'd just turned 18."

"You got married when you were 18?" The news is as liberating as it is dumbfounding. That means I can marry Noelle in just six years, seven if I wait to graduate high school!

My head spinning with possibility, Grandpa drops another bomb on me.

"Ever heard the story of how your mom and dad met?"

Everyone meets at some point in time. Until now, though, I never wondered how my parents came to know each another. But now that the topic has been breached...

"Well," Grandpa begins. "It all started when your old man was in need of a little help with his math."

"Ahem."

"Ah," Grandpa says. "Looks like your dad is here to tell it himself. I was just going to tell Adam and Michael here the story of you and Carol meeting and falling in love. But hey, since you're here, it only makes sense for you to take over. All I've told them is that you needed a math tutor. You can take it from here."

Dad gives Grandpa a raised eyebrow, crosses and uncrosses his arms, takes a step toward the straight-back chair only to walk past it and behind it, puts his forearms one over the other on top of the chair, places his weight on his forearms. He gazes at the floor, blows a hard breath out, and freezes.

I lean deep into the couch beside Grandpa. Look too interested and he might start prying about my own love life—and as you know, it's pretty juicy right now. But I'm not quite ready to share. Hey, it took years for Dad to tell me his story, and Noelle and I aren't even an official couple yet.

Big Mike obviously didn't get the memo to play it cool, because he looks like a lap dog about to be given his favorite treat. Fortunately, Dad doesn't notice.

"Yeah, I guess I needed a little help with numbers," Dad says. He's still staring at the floor, but he looks 15 years younger. He tussles his own hair, widens his eyes, and smiles at nothing. Unlike the maniacal smile that seems his MO these days, this is a genuine smile. One of pleasure. One of memory.

"Your mother, on the other hand—"

"Whoa, there, Darryl. Can't get to her just yet."

Dad is startled out of Memory Land and lands firmly in his father's living room.

"She wasn't the first one you went to for help adding and subtracting."

Dad looks quizzically at Grandpa, who returns the confused look.

"Come on!" Grandpa says. "You can't get straight to the good stuff. You've got to build up anticipation! Tell 'em about the flops you had at first, how desperate you were to find someone who actually knew what nine times twelve minus the square root of pi is."

"Yeah, yeah," Dad says finally. "As Grandpa said, your mother wasn't the first one I turned to for some math help. Tried quite a few others, actually. Probably five or six. I was starting to worry that there were no decent tutors at Kingsway University."

"That's right. Five or six, and none were any good."

"You going to let me finish, Gramps?"

"Sorry," Grandpa says. "Just glad you're giving some of the dirty details before getting to your prized possession."

Unable to hold it any longer, I laugh out loud.

It's comforting to see Grandpa and Dad interact this way, and I can't help but snicker at the whole thing.

Dad watches me and laughs some as well. Then he turns to Grandpa and asks permission to finish his story.

thirteen

"If you think you've got it rough, you've got another thing coming," Dad says. He's just told about the half dozen tutors he tried to no avail when he came upon an ad Mom put in the school library.

Math Help That Adds Up
Good Rates
Better Results
Ext. 137

Following a few successful tutoring sessions, Dad is so deeply in love he begins doing worse and worse in math. Which means he needs more tutoring help. Until he can't keep the cause of his declining math skills a secret any longer and asks the long-haired, fair-skinned math whiz on a date.

"You share a bedroom with your granddad?" Dad asks me. "Big deal. For your mother and my first date, I was so broke I made tomato soup." He pauses for drama.

"I love tomato soup," Big Mike says. "Did it have those little brown specks in it? Love those!"

"Tomato soup?" I ask to keep the story moving.

"Well, yeah," Dad recalls. "Of course, it wasn't really tomato soup. I'd taken a handful of ketchup packets from a local dive, squirted them into a pot, added a couple cups of water, warmed it up, and sprinkled a little pepper in there. That, young Shannon, was fine dining for a poor man like myself."

Grandpa leans back in his chair and chuckles.

"And you ate that?" I ask. "I mean—Mom ate that?" I've never seen her touch prepackaged anything, and the thought of her eating a poor man's "tomato" soup made out of ketchup packets and tap water is unthinkable.

"You better believe she ate it. Your mother actually thought it tasted quite good if I recall," Dad brags. "Though it could have benefited from another ketchup packet and a shake or two of basil."

"Yeah! Basil!"

We turn and stare at Big Mike.

"Basil," he repeats. "That's the brown speckled stuff Mom uses. Makes tomato soup taste amazing!"

Just then, Mom stumbles in. Her mascara is—no surprise—running down her face, a stark contrast to her well-put-together suit. She's obviously been interview hunting, and her lack of success follows her like a storm cloud.

The room is silent. As in: coffin silence.

Grandpa speaks up.

"Welcome home, Carol. Darryl here was just telling Adam how you two love birds met."

Mom shudders. She bites her lip and mopes to the kitchen.

Over the bang of pots, pans, forks, and knives, Dad and Grandpa find spots on the floor to stare at. I get flashbacks of when I brought up Mike's dad to him and his mom. With nowhere to put my eyes safely, I tell Mike I'll see him tomorrow and make my way to the bathroom.

"Good night, Mr. Carr and...Mr. Carr," Mike says.

"Good night, son," Grandpa says.

AND I SAVED THE WORLD

*****

It takes a while to fall asleep. When I wake up, Grandpa is smearing old-man deodorant on his pits and slipping on his signature shirt.

"Morning, Adam. Glad you're awake," he says. "I've been thinking about last night and have something special for you."

I want to respond, but my body won't let me. It knows it's Saturday, so it revolts. All I can do is stretch from head to foot, hands reaching stiffly over my head, back arched like an upside-down cat, mouth wide open in an oxygen-hungry yawn.

"Something special?" I finally ask, forcing my body to sit upright.

Grandpa walks to his dresser. With half his shirt buttoned, he opens the top drawer and pulls out the same box that caught my interest last night. He opens the box, grabs the huge class ring, smiles, and turns.

"Now, Adam, I want you to take good care of this. Your grandmother wouldn't want it to get damaged."

He drops the ring in my open hand.

"Grandpa...but...I thought you were going to sell it."

"Ah, who'd want to buy an old class ring? It

may be made of gold and have some fancy stone in it, but you can find that at any pawnshop around here. Besides," he continues, "Grandma would have wanted you to have it. She loved her Adam."

All my memories of Grandma were given to me by Grandpa—how she loved me, gave him the stink eye when we'd get into mischief, and how much I loved her cooking. While Grandma passed away before I could really know her, if she was anything as great as Grandpa, she was something else. But did I really want that ring?

"I do have some other things I need to sell though," Grandpa says. "Want to help?"

If there are gears inside my head, Grandpa can hear them moving faster than ever.

"Well?"

"Sure," I say excitedly. "I'd love to."

"Thought you would." Grandpa grabs a black cloth bag from the top shelf of his closet. "You had the look of an entrepreneur when I handed you that twenty a while back. So if you can get some stuff sold for me, I'll give you half of whatever you make. But your first task is to show me how to use this thing."

He sits down and pulls a laptop computer out of the bag. My grandfather is more high-tech than his

12-year-old grandson, but I don't have time to be embarrassed.

I stare at the small computer, doubting it has the right specs to play those games my lunch friends constantly talk about. But I can't spend too much time caring about that. This thing is going to fund my family's financial security.

"Looks pretty nice," I say. "Mind if I see it?"

"That's what I brought it out here for. Any idea how to get it up and running?"

A couple hours and three trips to the electronics store later, Grandpa's laptop is ready to make me rich. Thanks to the tech pros at Elektronix Town, I know how to use the computer's built-in camera, set up an email address, and post stuff for sale. Now to put some merchandise online and make some serious money.

"What did you want to sell, Grandpa?"

"Ah, you got the computer working?" He looks over his glasses and smiles. "Come with me, and I'll show you what trash I'd like to make another man's treasure."

In the kitchen, he opens a cabinet full of crystal, plastic cups, and salt-and-pepper shakers.

"Ta-da!"

I'M 12 YEARS OLD

My visions of becoming independently wealthy die a quick death.

"You want to sell this…stuff?"

"Yessir," Grandpa responds. "Unless you think you can't do it."

I roll my eyes at him. "Of course I can sell it. How much do you think I should sell all of it for?"

"That's up to you. You set the price," he says, pointing at me. "The more you sell it for, the more you make."

As Grandpa sits, I bring each item from the cabinet and place it on the kitchen table, mulling over what each piece can bring to my wallet. And then a banging on the front door takes my attention.

Big Mike is standing outside in shorts and a t-shirt.

"What are you, crazy?" I ask as I open the door.

Mike comes in trailed by a pipsqueak of a guy I don't even see until they're both in the living room. Startled, I jump back, thinking the stranger is a miniature home invader.

"Oh yeah," Mike says, "you've never met Z, have you? He's my cousin. Him and my aunt are gonna stay with us for a while."

"He and my aunt," I say under my breath.

"Huh?"

"Z your real name?"

The kid called Z looks at Mike.

"Good question," Mike says. "Is Z your real name?"

Z shrugs. Mike smiles.

"So…what you up to?" he asks.

I show Big Mike and Z the stuff Grandpa gave me to sell, tell them how he said I get to keep half the dough, laugh at the pitiful items at my disposal, but don't tell them why I'm doing it. Not that I don't like Big Mike or Quiet Z. Just don't want them spilling my secret family-saving plan to anyone else, so I keep it close to my chest.

At the end of the day, I place five items on eBay: an old-fashioned juicer made of metal and glass, a clear glass coffee mug with an image of Garfield and friends, a hideous crystal bowl that weighs at least 20 pounds, a gaudy metal nutcracker, and a wooden bowl with a flying eagle carved in the bottom.

Getting them online, however, is no easy feat, thanks to Big Mike. Every time I try to take a picture of something, he wants to hold it like Vanna White or force Z to look like he's using it happily—which is difficult with the scared look that's nailed to Z's face.

Somehow, I snap enough decent pictures to get the items online and up for auction. Now comes the waiting game.

My granddad kept these things around for years, so there has to be some old geezer who's interested in buying them so he can do the same. Or who knows? Maybe I could hit pay dirt and wind up with a bidding war between some hipsters who want a small metal nutcracker and a vintage Garfield glass at any price.

As I settle into bed, I'm entranced with my new online selling scheme. While the items aren't anything I would ever want to buy, there are stories of people making serious bank on trash that's worse than what I'm selling. And those big bucks are going to remind my parents that they love each other more than life itself.

That small bit of hope is all I need to forget about the bags growing darker and larger under Mom's eyes—or at least forget about them long enough to get to sleep.

fourteen

"Girls want a boy to do something romantic. But boys aren't too good at figuring out what's romantic and what's…not."

Almost out of earshot, I listen intently as she sounds out each word in a near whisper. Noelle, my queen who is yet unaware of her place in my life, is going on and on to her friends who cling to every word. It's as if every syllable is a new revelation, but if any of these girls had read the cover lines on any magazine in the grocery store checkout line, they would already know everything she has to say. As it is, they are as enamored with the information as I am the informer.

Oh, Noelle…

Then it hits me. The information Noelle shares isn't groundbreaking. But it will take my family-saving master plan to the next plateau. How have I not thought of this already?

After all the Shakespeare and Byron I read at the old house, waiting for Mom and Dad to get home when they had jobs, you'd think this would have been first on my mind. Suppose the extra dose of Dostoevsky and Vonnegut evened them out. Still, Grandpa and Dad handed me the solution to Mom and Dad's marital problems on a silver platter. How am I just picking up what they were laying down?

Great as it is that I have an epiphany, it doesn't lead to academic success. My daydreaming results in every teacher exacting revenge in the most teacherly way possible: they call on me. When I invariably stumble upon the correct answer, they each respond in their own way.

"Well done, Adam. Now if you could start looking like you're paying attention, we'll be in business."

"Glad to know there's something going on in that noggin of yours, Mr. Carr."

"Ha! Pulled another rabbit out of your hat, did you?"

"If only more folks had your ability to accidentally say the right word over and over."

At lunch, I grab a handful of ketchup packets. The lunch lady gives me a funny look. So do my lunch friends.

"Hey," I say, "I'm not the one wearing a hairnet."

Speaking of my lunch friends, I should probably introduce them. They're Sam, a red-headed kid with so many freckles his skin looks orange; Josh, who manages to have his shirt on backward half the time; and John, a guy who is thinner than me and thinks he has a future in MMA. Obsessed with video games, these three amigos think it's horrible that I can't play video games at home, but they hang out with me because I'm willing to hang out with them. Of course, if Big Mike had the same lunch period as I, there would be no need for the Nerd Herd.

Thankfully, though, they think I'm funny, and they perk up at my joke about the lunch lady's hairnet. They start laughing and the conversation turns from my ketchup-filled pockets to their sweet spot—video games.

"Maybe later," I say as I hop off the bus.

"Okay," Mike says. "Just let me know. We can hang out, work on the auction stuff...whatever you want to do."

"Sure thing, Mike."

The house is empty. Mom and Dad are probably job hunting and Grandpa is likely at the senior center playing bingo or doing old-people aerobics or keeping his brain strong. Wherever they are, they aren't home. Good news for me. I grab a medium-size pot and fill it halfway with water.

Two hours later, Mike and I sit on my bed with the door shut, wondering if a bidding war will erupt over the Garfield glass.

"If that thing doesn't sell for at least twelve bucks, I'll let you call me Tiny for a week."

I push Mike, but he doesn't budge. We laugh and he pushes me.

"The laptop!" I yell. Big Mike snags it out of my hand as I tumble to the floor with a nervous laugh.

He hands Grandpa's laptop back to me as the front door opens. I give his hands a double take. They look strange. Not quite small, but they look different. And either Big Mike's forearms have shrunk or mine have grown. I set the laptop on the bed and slide to the

78

closed bedroom door.

"What are you—"

"Shhhhhh!" I look hard at Mike with my finger firmly over my lips.

I listen as Dad's familiar, heavy steps stop at the couch. As part of his new post-interview routine, he drapes his sports coat over the back of the couch. Almost on cue, he sighs. On the other side of the door, I imagine him running his hands through his salt-and-pepper hair, which is getting longer than usual.

Then the routine breaks. Dad's slow footsteps cautiously lead him toward the kitchen. He laughs softly.

I let my breath go and suck in again as he thumbs the lighter I left on the table. I squeeze my eyes tight just in time to hear the flame grabbing hold of the candlewick.

But something is wrong. Very wrong.

"Mike!" I whisper. "What did you do? You're killing me! You smell like a sewage plant!"

Big Mike laughs in one hand like a girl and uses the other to fan away the stink.

A kitchen chair wheezes as Dad takes his seat. He taps the table with his fingers, taps the floor with his feet, fills the room with humming. A jazz tune.

"Your dad's got rhythm!"

"Be quiet, Mike! You whisper like a kindergartner."

Then the squeaking of the front door comes again. This time, it's followed by Mom's sad feet that drag her toward the kitchen. I picture her looking down, which is part of her new routine.

She stops moving.

"Darryl? What—what are you doing?"

"I'm not sure," I hear Dad say from the kitchen. "Looks like we'll be dining in candlelight though."

Mom's feet scoot forward with an ounce less moping.

"Is that…"

"Yeah." I'm pretty sure I hear Dad's head shake in disbelief. "Tomato soup. And looks like the executive chef did it the right way."

I picture Dad holding up the ketchup packet I left on the table.

"Tomato soup?" Big Mike says. "Why are we in here and letting them eat it all? I'm hungry!"

Right on cue, Mike's stomach growls low and fierce.

Then something odd happens. Something that hasn't happened for months—not since before the day

AND I SAVED THE WORLD

Mom came into my bedroom at our old house and told me Dad lost his job. A sound emits from my mother that is so sweet, so pure, so innocent, so lively, it would make hardened criminals cry. She laughs. Not a hearty guffaw or a slap-your-knee-and-scream howl. It is a nice, kind, gentle, I-love-saving-helpless-animals-and-embarrassing-my-son motherly laugh that says, "That boy of ours is something else."

And hey—who can blame her? That boy of hers is something else.

For an hour, I ignore all other senses to focus on the slight tinkering of spoon against bowl, light laughter, and quiet conversation.

Eventually, Mom and Dad rinse off their dishes and drop them in the sink. The front door opens and firmly closes.

"Mike."

The bulk on my twin mattress stirs and mumbles something.

"Hey, man," I say, nudging him. "It's late. Mom and Dad are gone, and you fell asleep. You should probably head home."

I crack open the bedroom door, sneak to the front door, and step outside.

Already half a block away, Dad walks tall, his

arm wrapped tightly around Mom. She nestles in the crook of his arm, their hot breath smoking in the cold air like the candle burning in the kitchen.

fifteen

There are two minutes left in the auction when Grandpa comes in.

"Ah, glad you're keeping watch over the store," he says. "What's on the chopping block?"

I pick up the pocketknife lying on the bed.

"Looks like folks are really into it," I say. "They were slowly upping the ante for a while, but it's heated up in the last hour."

Grandpa smiles and crosses his arms over his chest.

"Oh yeah. That beauty cut open many envelopes and—"

I wait for Grandpa to finish his sentence. He

grabs my left hand and then my right in both of his.

"Did you lose it?"

Whatever "it" is, I'm pretty sure Grandpa is the one who lost it.

"Lose what?"

"The ring, boy! The ring!"

"Oh," I say, relieved. "It's in my top drawer. Didn't want it getting lost."

Grandpa's body relaxes. His face returns to that of an elderly man who would give you any piece of candy you wanted so long as you ask politely.

He sits down as the front door bursts open. Grandpa and I both jump and look up. A wild-haired man stands like a wild-haired man should—suit on, tie crooked, smile of a serial killer across his face.

"I got an interview! I really got an interview!"

Grandpa walks purposefully, proudly into the living room and grabs Dad.

"I knew you'd get one, son. I just knew it!"

For the next fifteen minutes, Dad tells and re-tells the story of his happenchance meeting with an old friend, Julian Hart. Since graduating from high school decades earlier, Mr. Hart went from being a peace-loving environmentalist greenie to an attorney with save-the-planet leanings.

Because of his gentle demeanor and success rate in the courtroom, Mr. Hart's firm stays busy. So busy that they need to bring on a few new faces. Mr. Hart thinks Dad will be perfect for researching and finishing up some miscellaneous tasks that fall by the wayside. Not a glamorous job, but Dad doesn't care. Listening to him tell it, you'd think Dad was made President of the United States and his first task is to guarantee parents the right to give their children embarrassing names.

The interview is in a week, and within that time, Dad will probably go mad. Which means it was time for Adam Shannon Dakota Carr—again, for those not paying attention, that's me—to intervene.

However, I can't just toss some ketchup into hot water and assume it will turn into a hot date again. This time it's going to take all I have, which after a few decent online sales is exactly forty-five dollars and eighteen cents.

Of course, as expected I can't act on the plan yet. Thank you, pre-algebra homework.

sixteen

It's a long shot, but I need to interact with the most gorgeous girl ever to save my world at home. That's right. Noelle now factors into my save-the-world plans.

If only I'd read more of those romantic-type books or paid attention to the "What Women Want" articles in those old magazines. But, no! I go for the heady books filled with murder and the struggle of humanity and leave the love stuff for everyone else.

Oh well. It's for the family.

"Date night?"
My face burns when Noelle says it.

"Yeah," I finally say. "Date night. I just need you to write it down for me. You've got great penmanship. I mean, you're a girl, and girls are generally good at that kind of stuff."

Noelle turns to her friends and laughs.

"Date night, eh?"

"Yeah, date night. I'll give you a dollar if you do it. Please?"

Until that moment, I don't consider how strange it would be to ask the finest female on the planet to write "Date night" on a sheet of paper. Well, it's very strange. Not suave at all. It's even worse when you offer to pay her to do it. The word desperate comes to mind.

As soon as I get home, I grab my remaining cash and put it on the table where it can't be missed. Then I toss the note Noelle penned on top of it. In other words, I set the scene for a world-saving evening and settle down to watch it happen.

Sadly, I miss all the action. I guess the stress of all this stuff wore me out, because I don't realize I'm sleepy until I wake up.

"Adam! You in there?"

For such a big guy, Mike's brain is remarkably small. He's standing at my bedroom door looking at me, which makes me think the answer should be obvious. But apparently it's not.

"Yeah, Mike. What's up?"

"You ran off the bus so fast today. I was afraid something was wrong."

"No," I say with my eyes closed. "Everything's fine. Just had something I had to take care of."

I climb off the bed and shuffle into the living room. Big Mike follows.

The money is gone. I grab the note, which is still sitting on the table, and stuff it into my pocket for safe keeping.

"Date night?"

"Huh?"

Mike pokes me in the arm more gently than usual. "Saw the note. What's that all about?"

"I, uh…it's nothing. Something for my parents, I guess."

The clock reads 6:42 p.m. Mom and Dad are out having a night on the town, and it seems I'm left to my own devices for dinner. Nothing new, but it doesn't make it any less frustrating.

"Hungry?" I finally ask Mike.

AND I SAVED THE WORLD

Everything I need for a quick dinner is missing from the pantry. There's no peanut butter. No jelly. No bread.

"Looking for something?"

"Grandpa!" I yell. "Where'd you come from? You scared me half to death!"

"This is my house," Grandpa says, "and we share a bedroom—my bedroom. It's only natural that you would forget about me being here."

"Yeah, Adam," Big Mike says, "it's only natural."

I roll my eyes at Big Mike and Grandpa.

Grandpa pushes the PB&J in front of an empty chair and motions for me to sit down. Then he gets up and grabs the milk from the refrigerator, pours a couple glasses, slides one in front of me and the second in front of an empty chair.

"You gonna eat, Michael?" Grandpa asks.

"Oh, I don't want to—"

"So you're going to stand there and stare at us like a starving wolf?" Grandpa laughs. "Sit down and eat. You're a growing boy."

"Thanks, Mr. Carr. I love peanut butter and jelly."

Is there anything that big ol' boy doesn't love to

eat? Big Mike spreads peanut butter on one piece of bread, jelly on the other, and jams the two together. He holds it up to inspect, and I realize he truly does love peanut butter and jelly.

I take a bite of my not-so-appreciated sandwich.

"Anything happening with Noelle these days?" Grandpa asks.

I nearly choke.

"Noelle?" I pretend I can't place the name. Look at the ceiling for the answer. Isn't there. Look at Mike, but he's not paying attention. He's on Peanut Butter and Jelly Planet. Look at Grandpa and shrug. Grandpa isn't buying my story. But he doesn't harp on it.

Instead, he skips to the living room and flips on the TV.

"You in?"

For the first time since we started sharing a bedroom, Grandpa beats me at Wheel of Fortune and Jeopardy!—so yeah, I guess my head is swirling a little. The hardest part is struggling to think of three things at once: Noelle, the date I sent my parents on, and what I can pull off the walls at Grandpa's house to sell. Tack on Big Mike yelling the wrong answer for each and every puzzle and the wrong question to every answer and you can easily see why I feel like

AND I SAVED THE WORLD

I'm cracking.

seventeen

Mom is finishing breakfast as I stumble into the kitchen.

"Morning, Shannon!"

"Yup."

When I pass her, I give her a double take. She's not been awake this early in months. Her mascara isn't running for the hills and she doesn't look like she just heard the world is going to end.

"Surprised to see me?"

Understatement of the century.

"Yeah," I say. "Guess I—guess I am. It's…pretty early."

"Well, I've got some exciting news. Your father

isn't the only one with a job prospect. Your mother here," she says, striking a glamour pose, "is entering the wide world of education."

I rack my brain. Education…education…

"I'm going to be a substitute teacher!"

"A sub?"

"Yes, 'a sub.' I dropped by your school a few weeks ago to ask your principal about—"

"You stopped where?" My heart sinks. The sun goes black.

"Palmetto Middle! Well," she continues, oblivious to my suffocation, "your principal and I got to talking, and wouldn't you know, they need more substitute teachers! Well, I've never done such a thing, but I thought, 'Why not? I can manage a few middle school students for a few hours.' I have, after all, managed you all these years. May even change the world!"

By the looks of things, she is definitely subbing today. She's wearing flat-bottom brown shoes with a long skirt, a plain button-up shirt with a small pink cardigan over top, and her hair is in a substitute teacher bun.

I swallow.

"Who you subbing for today?"

The question lingers. Decades pass.

"Don't worry, dear," Mom says. "I doubt very much I would wind up in one of your classes."

Oxygen overwhelms my lungs. Birds begin chirping outside. A rainbow crosses the sky. Make that a double rainbow.

"Today I'm covering for the typing teacher." Mom looks at me. "I don't believe you're in typing class this semester, are you, sweetheart?"

"No," I say, almost weeping for joy. "I'm not taking typing right now."

Fueled by thankfulness, I scarf down the biggest breakfast I've eaten in months, get dressed for school, and am almost outside to wait for the bus when Mom yells for me.

"Shannon—you don't have to ride the bus today. I'm going there, too," she says. "We can ride together!"

Clouds return overhead but aren't all gloom and doom. After all, I can run from her as soon as we arrive at school. As an added plus, I don't have to ride the bus. Since Big Mike hasn't been on The Big Cheese in a while, I've lost my priority seating, so I'm definitely game for skipping a day of bus riding.

"Can I pick the music on the way?" I ask.

*****

AND I SAVED THE WORLD

When we get to school, escaping my mother's grip is a cinch. As I bolt from the car, she is still staring in the rearview mirror, checking her lipstick and hair.

Inside, I toss my stuff in my locker, grab what I need for first period, and head to homeroom. The Nerd Herd is already there, talking about the newest video game I'll never play.

"Hey, Adam," John says. "We were just talking about—well, stuff you don't care about."

"Let me guess," I say with a smirk. "Video games?"

If I let them know I actually want to play the video games I don't have access to, I'll be the weirdo for a totally different reason.

I can hear it now, blaring over the PMS intercom system:

"Attention: students. Will the skinny, unmuscular, long-haired son of two Earth-saving environmentalists who is not permitted to spend his time playing video games and who spends lots of time reading classic literature his father keeps around the house as homage to his English degree come to the office? His parents are here to get him."

I'd much rather be the weird guy who thinks

video games are a waste of time.

Homeroom is uneventful as usual, and when the bell rings, I'm ready to get on with whatever the day has to offer. I say my goodbyes to Sam, Josh, and John, avoid a near collision with a couple talking girls, and slip into the hall.

On the way to math class, someone keeps yelling "Shannon" over and over. I don't flinch until I feel a grab at my shoulder from behind. It's Mom, and she's panting.

"Goodness! Didn't think I'd ever get to you."

Mom's once-perfect hair is already disheveled, which does not bode well for the rest of the day. She looks like she has run into every student in the entire school.

"Is it always this hectic in the hallways? People are everywhere!"

"Uh, yeah, Mom, it's middle school."

"Well, I just wanted to say hello and that I will see you at the end of the day!"

And she's off, down the hall and up the stairs to take the helm in front of the day's typing classes.

"Mr. Carr, I hope you don't plan to stand there all day."

"No, sir," I tell The Glowing Orb. "I'm getting

to class right now."

Through PMS's front door, I see a large-framed kid get escorted to a car by his mom. She looks like Mike's mom, but that kids' large frame is missing the Big Mike swagger. Must be someone else. And I need to get to class.

First period is full of the norm: fractions, decimal points, X's, Y's, multiplying, trains traveling from two different directions at different speeds. Second is typical as well. Third period—that's where things get interesting. Or for my classmates, entertaining.

It starts before the bell even rings. Sniggering, pointing, mouth holding in an attempt to hide laughter.

"So you weighed 11 pounds when you were born?"

The ice is broken by Damien Childress, a former wallflower. Thanks to a patchy peach-fuzz mustache, he gained the adoration of a cluster of girls and jumped from nobody to somebody over night.

I ignore him.

"Shannon—I'm talking to you!"

"What?"

I look around, acting like I'm trying to figure out who Shannon is. His pointing finger, however, leaves no question.

"Shannon Carr, you weighed 11 pounds when you were born." The recently converted wallflower leans back in his chair and massages his peach fuzz. "That's a lot of baby."

A small group surrounding him laughs heartily.

Great. Here we go again. All the safety of my new school is being thrown out the window. It's sink or swim. I've never wished Big Mike were here more than now.

"Yeah, I was a little hefty," I say. "You must have gone through quite a bit of trouble to get your hands on that bit of intelligence."

"Not really," Fuzz answers. "Your mom told us in class this morning."

My mother? The woman I gave my money to so she and Dad could go out on a date?

"Had us type it, actually. 'Adam Shannon Dakota Carr is my only child,'" Mustache mimics. "'When I went into labor, the doctors didn't know if I could birth his large head and body.'"

As Damien speaks, Noelle cowers, a look of panic and fear on her every feature. Next to her, a cluster of goons fake puke all over the floor, their desks, and whatever else is in puking proximity.

AND I SAVED THE WORLD

"Okay everyone, let's get to work."

For the first time, I am enthralled with The Glowing Orb's invigorating lesson on proper language usage.

eighteen

I'm awake before my alarm starts buzzing. Fully dressed, I sprint to the bathroom and scrub my teeth carefully. (A guy needs good breath for the ladies, even if his dad doesn't have a job and seems to be losing his mind.) After wiping my mouth, I duck into my room and grab my book bag, speed walk to the front door, grab the handle.

"Shannon!"

Sometimes being scared makes you run, but this time I'm frozen still. Following an eternity of immobility, I crane my neck to see Dad leaning against the kitchen wall.

"Hey, Dad," I say. "See ya later."

"Whoa, there!" He holds out his hand like a cop directing traffic and walks toward me. "Thought I'd give you a lift since you're running late for the bus."

"I'm not running la—"

"Okay, okay," he says, "you're actually early. I thought we could do breakfast together. Hoping for the big interview today and breakfast is the most important meal—right?"

Somehow, Dad finds time for us to sit down at a diner for breakfast. I eat while he talks big plans with his mouth and accents them with his hand motions. By the time we pull up to school, I'm so thankful to get away from Mr. Interview that I forget to remind Dad to call me by my boy name.

"See you after school, Shannon!" Dad yells as I climb the front steps.

A horde of eighth graders turn their heads in unison. I am immediately transformed into road kill. Because I'm no longer an unknown sixth grader. I am now Shannon, the boy with the girl name.

"What did he say?"

I look up in response to the angry voice, the mocking voice, the last voice I expect to hear before meeting my maker. But no one is looking at me. The whole group is staring at my dad, who is still waving.

"Who you calling Shannon, old man?" a wiry eighth grader yells out. "I ain't no girl!"

The choke collar on his neck and heavy mascara on his eyes tell a different story, but I don't have time to argue, so I keep moving.

A leaning tower of books falls out of my locker just as I hear the tardy bell. Grabbing my books for first and second period, I slam my locker shut with my elbow. I pause, realizing my combination lock is in my hand, but figure my locker is safe for a couple hours and stumble toward homeroom.

"Adam, you're late."

My homeroom teacher, Ms. Stacklin, has a way of stating the obvious.

"Yes, ma'am," I reply. I dump my math and grammar books in my chair and approach her desk to explain.

Ms. Stacklin's left eyebrow is cocked, prepared for whatever story I throw her way.

"My dad," I say. "It's his fault. He wanted to eat breakfast with me and I couldn't say no because he—well…I just couldn't say no."

Behind me, the class is growing louder.

"Class, quiet down!" Ms. Stacklin screeches

over my shoulder. "Got a note?"

I feel through my pants pockets for a note that doesn't exist. "No, ma'am," I begin. "I didn't realize I was late."

Big Mike isn't at school today again. He's not been around for a week or so, and the rumor mill is in full effect.

The most impressive and probable excuse is that he got kicked out of school again for fighting. If you're upset at me for not telling you he's something of a fighter, I did it with the best of intentions. No reason to have you judge the guy based on his right hook.

Anyway, he very well may have gotten kicked out for fighting. Around here, a lot of troublemakers wind up in alternative school. It's basically a school filled with other kids who fight a lot and never show up for class. When they get sent to alternative school, they get to practice their delinquent skills together, while their teachers try to get them to care about long division.

In most areas of the civilized world, alternative school is offered only to high school students. However, the fine folks who run our school district wanted the local hoodlums to have more time to fraternize with one another, so they get them started early.

Word in the middle school hallway, however, is bigger than alternative school. The story is that when Mike got kicked out, his mom decided to send him to a military academy.

For those who are unfamiliar, military school is essentially like being in the military and school at the same time. Hence the clever name. You wake up super early, get yelled at all day, have to clean toilets with your toothbrush if your bed isn't made properly, and do all kinds of other fun stuff.

Without Michael Jackson around, I almost blend into the background at PMS. I'm suddenly forced to try to make more friends, but it doesn't go too well. Whatever the cause of Mike's disappearance, there's a Big Mike-sized hole in my life. At a new school, a guy's gotta have a best friend. When he's the biggest, baddest dude around, life is pretty nice. Take him away and suddenly, well—I feel like I'm going to have to figure out how to relate to those video game-playing lunch pals a bit better.

Believe it or not, first and second periods are a breeze. Third period isn't as bad as it could have been. I didn't do my homework, but the teacher is absent. Thankfully, we get the best sub in the world: Mr. Kirk. He's not the best because he ensures vigorous academic study in the classroom. Quite the opposite. Mr. Kirk knows he gets paid to babysit. In my book, he's the best babysitter around, because he lets us do whatever we want as long as we don't interfere with his daily dose of smartphone web surfing. Well, I'm not going to keep him from staring at a screen the size of his palm.

I sit back and watch small groups of kids talk about which boys or girls they like, which boys or girls they hate, how the basketball team should have won last night, and whatever else middle school kids talk about when left to their own devices. I even talk with a couple of them, mainly because they want to hear stories of Big Mike. So I give them stories, making him larger than life (which isn't that hard) and imagine what he's doing at military academy right now.

When a couple guys leave the classroom with bathroom passes in their hands, I figure I should do the same when they return. Otherwise, if The Glowing Orb is here for English, I'll be holding it for another 45 minutes. Getting a bathroom pass from The Orb is as likely as wetting your pants during class without anyone knowing it.

The bathroom boys return and hand the passes to Mr. Kirk, who doesn't give them a look. They laugh their way back to their desks.

"Be back in a few," I say. I cut my Big Mike story short and head to the front of the class.

"I need to go to the bathroom."

I expect a no-look hand-off of the bathroom pass, the same hand-off Mr. Kirk gave the Goof Troop. Instead, he looks like I ruined his day.

"You're going to have to wait," he says, looking at his watch. "Bell's about to ring and I need to give out homework. Don't worry," he says, attempting to use the sarcastic and authoritative tone regular teachers employ. "You'll have three minutes between classes to use it."

The bathroom boys are still laughing and whispering to anyone who will gather around.

"All right, everybody," Mr. Kirk shouts over the noise. "You don't have any homework—unless you didn't do your homework last night."

He mumbles something else, but the bell rings too loudly to hear him.

As everyone sprints out of the room, I place all my hope on The Glowing Orb being out. I didn't do my grammar homework last night, and ever since I asked to go to the bathroom, my brain decided I really need to use it.

I sprint down the hall, up the stairs, and down the hallway to second period and make a mental note to talk with the principal about laying out the school a bit better. As soon as I step over the threshold, the bell rings. The Orb is—unfortunately—not absent. He's already at the board, finishing a fifth sentence we have to diagram.

I know it's pointless, but I rush to his side and ask if I can go to the bathroom.

"Should have gone between classes," he says. Slapping the period at the end of the final sentence on the board, he gives me a brief smile and turns to the class. "Everyone in your seats, please. Copy these sentences and begin diagramming them. Once you've done that, raise your hand and I'll come check your work."

I stay by his side, doing my best pee-pee dance.

"Okay, Mr. Carr. You may go to the restroom, but please hurry."

"Yes, sir."

Bathroom pass in hand, I take off down the hall. Little does The Orb know my bathroom of choice is on the first floor, so he'll have to loan me a few minutes to get there and back. If he ever had to use the second floor boys' room he would understand.

I reach the stairwell and hop on the railing for a quick ride down. When I land at the bottom, I pause. The space feels smaller.

I look left, right, down, and then up. There is something hanging from the ceiling. A few things, actually. I wonder how I missed them when I sprinted to class.

Walking forward, I squint my eyes into focus. The things hanging from the ceiling look like clothes.

"Impossible," I whisper.

I always leave a couple pair of tighties in my locker for gym class. The gym teacher has a strict no-boxer policy. But there is no way they could be—

"Shannon Carr?"

I turn around, shaking. The choke-collared, mascara-wearing eighth grader who yelled at my dad that morning is standing behind me, punching his right fist into his open left hand. My gaze returns to the hanging underwear, SHANNON CARR written in perfect capital letters by my oh-so-helpful dad.

"You're Shannon, are you? Well, you're gonna die!" The mascara around his eyes suddenly makes him look less feminine and more ferocious. There is only one thought in my head, and it goes a little like this: I am about to die at the hands of a make-up-wearing guy who could have benefited from a few more hugs when he was a child.

Without thinking any more, I dart down the hall, run past my wide-open locker, and turn right. Each time I hear my name, I run faster, more determined to survive.

Ripping the bathroom door open, I'm overwhelmed with regret. Why didn't I book it to the office, where I'd be safe, where responsible adults would protect me? But it's too late. My body forced me into the bathroom, and I will have to face my maker a few years ahead of schedule, in a decades-old middle school boys' bathroom that smells like a decades-old middle school boys' bathroom.

Since the stalls don't have doors, I stand in the open and wait. The bathroom door flies open. Instead of the dirty black leather boots of Mr. Mascara, there is a pair of brown leather penny loafers. Linked to the shoes is Mr. Confetti, the school vice principal.

He pushes his hair out of his eyes and leans against the first sink. As he catches his breath, he points a finger at me.

"Why were you running?" he gasps. "I was yelling for you and you took off!"

"Er…sorry, sir."

"Where were you going anyway? And why is your underwear hanging from the lights down the hall?"

I want to answer, but I don't know how. I don't have conversations about my undies dangling from the fluorescent lights in the PMS hallway every day.

"Well, doesn't matter now," he says. "Your dad's here. Says you left your lunch in his car and something about your mom wanting you to eat what she packs because it's healthier than cafeteria food. The office tried paging you in English class, but you weren't there. I started looking for you when I saw you running down the hall."

"My dad brought my lunch?" The horns on Dad's head are replaced with a halo. At the same time I mentally saint Dad, I let out a sigh of relief that he didn't walk to English class and hand me the lunch bag in person.

"So, go on then," Mr. Confetti says, shooing me with his hands. "Get to the office and pick up your lunch. And don't worry about your unders. I'll have the janitor take them down."

110

nineteen

Since I'm the one writing the story, I'm going to write it like I wish it had happened. No, I'm not going to make stuff up to make myself look better than I actually am. Doing that would take an incredible imagination. I am, however, going to skip the boring stuff.

Thanks to me, you don't have to sit through parent-teacher conferences during which my proud mother nods in agreeance with everything every teacher says, because, after all, she, too, is a teacher of sorts and understands the difficulties teachers have on a daily basis. You also don't have to read about how my online business ends when I learn that the people buying the stuff I put online are Grandpa's friends whom he pays to make me think I'm doing something useful. And you don't have to suffer through my countless blown opportunities to become the knight in shining armor that Noelle so desperately needs.

Nope. I'm skipping all that and pushing you straight to the action. Welcome to the end of the school year. If you've missed my old pal Big Mike, you're not alone. One of the rumors must be true, because I've not seen him since before Mom started subbing.

I drop by Big Mike's house and bang on the door every few days, but no one ever answers. It's weird, but what can I do? I don't have his phone number. Don't know if he even has a cell phone. Besides, Mike can take care of himself. If only I could.

With Big Mike gone, I'm lost. At first, I try to assert myself and maintain the small position of power I inherited as his long-haired sidekick. While it works for a little while, most people aren't giving me the time of day. So I go out of my way to become unseen. When you've got hair to your shoulders and your mom is always screaming how much she loves you while she goes to another sub job, it ain't easy. But I work at it and it pays off for the most part. Hence why we're skipping ahead. Me not doing anything except avoiding the spotlight is not that exciting.

AND I SAVED THE WORLD

By this time, Dad is settled into his job. He runs errands and performs painfully tedious research for snooty lawyers, and he loves it. It gives him purpose, makes him feel he is part of something bigger than himself: the law. To be honest, it is cool to tell people my dad works for a hotshot attorney. Of course, the cool factor drops when they find out my dad isn't an attorney, but hey, I'll take cool anywhere I can get it.

Anyway, with the end near, it is time for end-of-course tests, a.k.a. EOCs. It's basically a way to show how great a job the teachers do and how smart the students are. Unfortunately, over the years the tests stopped reaping the results the school board wanted. Kids are failing. Miserably.

Since raises are based on student performance, teachers have all but given up on getting paid more.

While we're on the subject of sad stuff, EOCs are taken in our homeroom classrooms. Guess whose mom is subbing for his homeroom teacher?

For an entire week (yes, they force us to fill in bubbles for five whole days), I am stuck in a torture chamber inside my sixth grade homeroom. My desk is no longer a place to relax and get caught up on school gossip before the day starts. It has been transformed into something worse than an electric chair, a place where I cannot escape tales of the world's most embarrassing storyteller.

"Adam, have you told your friends about your first trip to Disney World? You were so scared!"

"Adam, I've never heard you talk about girls. You do like them, don't you?"

"Adam, your skin is looking so much better! I'm so glad that acne cream took care of that pimple for you!"

It's becoming too much. I know—I shouldn't complain. In a world full of poverty and brokenness, I have it easy. But I challenge anyone to sit in my home-room chair for one day. Even one hour.

In the midst of such challenges, a miracle occurs. On the final day of EOCs, my plan to save the world comes to fruition, courtesy of my embarrassing parents.

Mom sits in front of the class, watching us fill in bubbles. She giggles occasionally, most likely thinking of new stories to share with my classmates. Stories of my uncanny ability as an infant to fill a diaper immediately after Mom put a new one on me. Tales of my short-lived love affair with having my hair permed. Play-by-plays of my reaction when I learned Santa doesn't squeak down the chimney and stuff presents under the tree. Meanwhile, my hand is killing me. I've filled in 4.3 million ovals over the course of the week, and I can't take much more.

"Okay, guys, that's it," Mom says in her best teacher voice. "Put your pencils down and pass up your tests. And no talking until all tests are turned in."

A collective sigh fills the room. Mom stands in front of a row of students, waiting for tests to be placed in her hand.

The moment Mom grabs the last stack of EOCs, the class erupts with talking, laughing, and singing. A couple guys stand up and do goofy dances, others pump their fists in the air victoriously. It is sheer pandemonium.

With all the noise, it's impossible to hear the door open, but suddenly Dad is by Mom's side. She leans against the teacher's desk, listens to every word as if Dad is Walt Whitman or Winston Churchill, and she begins doing what she's not done since starting this substitute teacher thing. She cries.

The entire class stares at the front of the room, where Mom and Dad stand hugging and crying.

Mom waves to me, so I scurry to the desk.

"Tell him, Darryl."

"They want me to stay at the firm," Dad says.

"They want me to become a legal writer. Actually put my English degree to use. I won't be writing the great American novel, but it's a job with words. We're going to be okay, Adam. We're going to be okay!"

Dad looks at Mom. It's one of those I'm-going-to-kiss-you-right-now-even-though-our-son-is-going-to-be-totally-grossed-out-and-embarrassed-for-the-rest-of-his-life looks. Then he follows through.

"Oh, come on!" I yell, shielding my face and hiding my smile. "I just threw up a little in my mouth!"

When I remember I'm standing in front of the class, I cross my fingers, hold my breath, and wish my way to another galaxy.

It doesn't work.

The class looks at us with a mixture of horror, confusion, and on one face—the only one that matters, the face of an angel named Noelle who will one day be all mine—love.

So Mom and Dad are together and happy, Dad's got a job, and—well…we're still living with Grandpa, but he's a pretty cool roommate. If only he didn't snore.

As I consider the taste of swallowed vomit, something jabs my thigh. I reach into my pocket and pull out Grandpa's old class ring. I slip it on and off every finger on my right hand until I find one that looks about right. It will need a little tape on the bottom to fit, but I think it will work out.

twenty

Okay, okay. I know what you're thinking. The book title is a bit misleading. I didn't exactly save the world. Dad seemed to do put things back in order with some help from an old friend. I did help a little though.

Anyway, I bet you were concerned that the technology-less underdog didn't have a chance in this fight. You probably thought things would end up pretty bad for me. Well, my reading friends, you were wrong.

Don't take it personally, though. I did get my tighties strung across the overhead lights at school and my parents kissed in front of my entire homeroom class. So I guess you get the last laugh. For now…

sneak peak

What happens to Big Mike?

Find out in **I'm 13 Years Old And I Changed The World**— out now by Sir Brody Books!

Look below for the first chapter.

one

I ride home with Mom after school, still a bit shocked. Dad has a job, Mom and Dad kissed in front of my entire class, Noelle was touched by my parents' smooch, and the school year is over. It's a lot to take in, and I ride in silence trying to figure out which part is most worthy of my attention.

But it's no use. I think of all of them at once, my brain hopping from the kiss to Dad's new job to Noelle's look of "Aaaahhh!" and back again. As we approach Grandpa's driveway, an ambulance pulls up to Big Mike's. Its lights are on, but the sirens are silent.

The back doors pop open and an EMT hops out and helps another inside the ambulance lower a stretcher to the sidewalk.

Mrs. Jackson climbs out and holds the arm of a thin creature who looks vaguely familiar.

I wave.

A weak voice calls out from the stretcher.

"Adam! Hey, man—school out?"

"Yeah, school's out," I say, unsure whose voice it is.

I move toward the stretcher.

Mrs. Jackson smiles.

I look down.

Wearing a powder blue hospital gown is a creature that was once the terror of PMS.

"Mike?"

To be continued....

ABOUT THE AUTHOR

D.K. Brantley writes in his dining room, kitchen, bedroom, living room, and basement. He has even spent a fair amount of time writing in the food court of his local mall. He lives in Cleveland, Tennessee, with his wife, their two children, and a miniature Schnauzer.

OTHER BOOKS BY D.K. Brantley

I'm 13 Years Old And I Changed The World

Big Mike has cancer, and I've got to step in and do what science hasn't yet done. I've got to find a cure.

That's right—I'm 13 years old, and I'm about to change the world.

Illustrated by Ekaterina Khozatskaya

The Only Magic Book You'll Never Need

Not for the faint of heart, weak of knee, incontinent of bladder, or student of Hogwarts, this book teaches you to cauterize a severed torso, turn friends into enemies using super glue and headphones, and more. Becoming an illusionist has never been so impossible, dangerous, or funny.

CPSIA information can be obtained
at www.ICGtesting.com
Printed in the USA
BVHW03203291119
565094BV00003B/232/P

9 780692 399798